Near and Far

Luana Mitten and Meg Greve

ROURKE PUBLISHING

Vero Beach, Florida 32964

www.rourkepublishing.com

PHOTO CREDITS: © Glenda Powers: 3; © Jane Norton: 4, 5; © Gene Chutka: 6, 7; © Rick Rhay: 8; © Ana Abejon: 9; © Steven Phraner: 10, 11; © Justin Horrocks: 12, 13; © mandygodbehear: 14, 15; © Harry Hu: 16; © Nathan Gleave: 17; © Sergei Popov: 18; © Yiannos Ioannou: 19; © Joselito Briones: 20, 21; © Carmen Martínez Banús: 22, 23

Editor: Luana Mitten

Cover design by Nicola Stratford, bdpublishing.com

Interior Design by Tara Raymo

Library of Congress Cataloging-in-Publication Data

Mitten, Luana K.
  Near and far / Luana Mitten and Meg Greve.
      p. cm. -- (Concepts)
  Includes bibliographical references and index.
  ISBN 978-1-60694-384-7 (alk. paper) (hardcover)
  ISBN 978-1-60694-516-2 (softcover)
  ISBN 978-60694-574-2 (bilingual)
  1. Space perception--Juvenile literature. I. Greve, Meg. II. Title.
  BF469.M58 2010
  423'.12--dc22
                        2009016025

Printed in the USA

CG/CG

www.rourkepublishing.com - rourke@rourkepublishing.com
Post Office Box 643328 Vero Beach, Florida 32964

Near and far,
far and near,
what's the difference
between near and far?

3

4

My school is near.
I'll ride my bike.

5

My grandma is far.
I'll go by plane.

6

The park is near.
I think I'll skip.

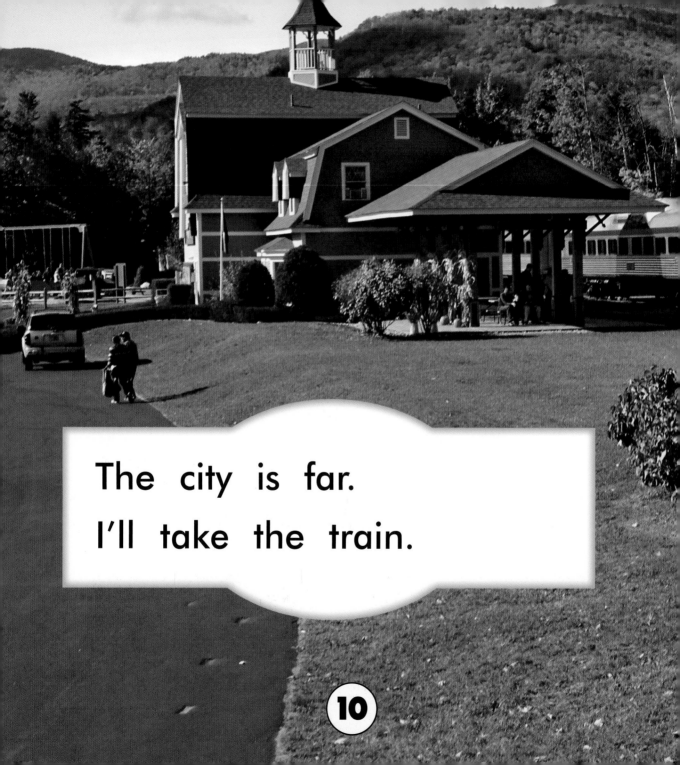

The city is far.
I'll take the train.

The store is near.
I'll take a walk.

The museum is far.
I'll go by car.

The second floor is near.
I'll take the stairs.

The top floor is far.
I'll take the elevator!

18

What is near?

What is far?

23

Index

Websites to Visit

pbskids.org/rogers/R_house/speedydelivery/speedy.html

www.timeforkids.com/TFK/kids/news/story/0,28277,524748,00.html

www.nhtsa.dot.gov/people/injury/pedbimot/bike/
    KidsandBikeSafetyWeb/images/KidsandBikeSafety.pdf

About the Authors

Thanks to phone calls and e-mails, Meg Greve and Luana Mitten can work together even though they live about 1,200 miles (1,900 kilometers) apart. Meg lives in the big city of Chicago, Illinois and gets to play in the snow with her kids. Luana lives on a golf course in Tampa, Florida and gets freckles on her face from playing at the beach with her son.

Artist: Madison Greve